C0-AJQ-712

海豚双语童书经典回放
**Classical Playback of Dolphin
Bilingual Children's Books**

Dream-Buyer

买梦

海豚出版社
DOLPHIN BOOKS
CIPG 中国国际出版集团

图书在版编目（CIP）数据

买梦：汉英对照 / 赵冰波改编. −− 北京：海豚出版社, 2015.3

（海豚双语童书经典回放）

ISBN 978−7−5110−1481−8

Ⅰ. ①买… Ⅱ. ①赵… Ⅲ. ①儿童文学—图画故事—中国—当代 Ⅳ. ①I287.8

中国版本图书馆CIP数据核字(2015)第035182号

书　　名：海豚双语童书经典回放·买梦
作　　者：赵冰波

总发行人：俞晓群

责任编辑：李忠孝　陈三霞　李宏声
责任印制：王瑞松
出　　版：海豚出版社有限责任公司
网　　址：http://www.dolphin-books.com.cn
地　　址：北京市西城区百万庄大街24号
邮　　编：100037
电　　话：010-68997480（销售）　010-68998879（总编室）
传　　真：010-68998879
印　　刷：北京捷迅佳彩印刷有限公司
经　　销：新华书店及网络书店
开　　本：16开（710毫米×960毫米）
印　　张：1.375　字　　数：5千
印　　数：5000
版　　次：2015年3月第1版　　2015年3月第1次印刷
标准书号：ISBN 978-7-5110-1481-8
定　　价：17.00元

版权所有　侵权必究

买梦
Dream-Buyer

One day, Frog was perched on a big lotus leaf in the middle of the lake. He looked this way and that, busy looking for insects to eat.

Red Bird flew up and happily told him: "Hello, Frog, let me tell you something. Last night I had a dream. In the dream I played with a beautiful butterfly."

Frog blinked his eyes and thought that was wonderful.

有一天,小青蛙自个儿蹲在湖里的大荷叶上,东张西望,忙着找虫子吃。

一只小红鸟飞来了,很高兴地对小青蛙说:"小青蛙,告诉你吧,我昨天晚上做了一个梦,梦见和一只好漂亮的大蝴蝶一起玩呢!"

小青蛙眨眨眼睛,心想:哟,这可真好!

After the little red bird left, Yellow Bird flew up, "Guess what, Frog, I dreamed last night that I saw a marigold. It was so beautiful!"
Frog blinked again: That's great...

小红鸟飞走了。小黄鸟又飞来了，对小青蛙说："小青蛙，告诉你吧，我昨天晚上做了一个梦，梦见一朵孔雀花，美极了！"

小青蛙又眨眨眼睛，心想：哟，真好……

And then Yellow Bird flew away.

Frog thought to himself, "Dreaming is beautiful. Tonight I want to have an interesting dream."

When night fell, Frog got down in the mud very early. He closed his eyes and waited for a dream to come. He waited, and waited, and slowly he fell asleep.

But, he didn't dream.

小黄鸟说完，就飞走了。

小青蛙想：呀，做梦真美。今天晚上，我也要做一个好玩的梦。

到了晚上，他早早地趴在泥沼里，闭上眼睛，等着梦来。小青蛙等啊，盼呀，慢慢睡着了。

可是他没有做梦。

After he woke up, he closed his eyes and thought: "Why, I didn't dream." He was very unhappy.

Suddenly, he got an idea: "I know, I'll go buy a dream."

So he took a penny and went off to buy a dream.

Frog lept from lotus leaf to lotus leaf. When he saw Redcarp swimming in the water he called out, "Redcarp, Redcarp, do you have any spare dreams? I'd like to buy one."

"No, I don't." Redcarp turned and swam off, her red tail fin wagging in the green water.

小青蛙一觉醒来，闭着眼睛想了想：咦？我什么梦也没做呀。他很不高兴。

突然，小青蛙想到一个好主意："对了，我去买一个梦吧！"

小青蛙在荷叶上跳来跳去，看到红鲤鱼在水里游。他对红鲤鱼说："红鲤鱼，红鲤鱼，我想买一个梦，你有吗？"

红鲤鱼说："我没有。"说完，红鲤鱼游走了。她那红红的尾巴，在绿绿的湖水里一甩一甩的。

Just then, Swan floated down onto the water. Frog hurried over to her. "Swan, Swan, I want to buy a dream. Have you got any?"

"I don't sell dreams." Swan answered, then flew up into the air. Her broad white wings fluttered across the blue sky.

这时候，几只白天鹅落到水面上，小青蛙急忙跳过去，对白天鹅说："天鹅，天鹅，我想买个梦，你有吗?"

白天鹅说："我不卖梦。"说完，白天鹅扇着翅膀向天上飞去。她那雪白的大翅膀，在蓝蓝的天空中一扇一扇的。

Frog came to the shore of the lake. Little White Bunny was playing on a swing.

"Little White Bunny, would you please sell me some dreams?" Frog asked.

"How can I sell my dreams to you?" answered Little White Bunny and went back to swinging on the swing. She swang higher and higher and looked like a white cloud floating in the sky.

Frog couldn't buy a dream so he went sadly home.

小青蛙又来到湖边,看到小白兔在岸上的树林里荡秋千。

小青蛙大声说:"小白兔,小白兔,我想买一个梦,你有吗?"

小白兔说:"我的梦怎么能卖给你呢?"说完,又荡起秋千来。她荡呀,荡呀,好像一朵白云在飘。

小青蛙买不到梦,难过地回家去了。

Night fell. Frog thought, "I didn't buy a dream. There certainly won't be any dreams tonight."

The night was quiet. Frog breathed lightly in and out and quickly fell asleep.

And then, he started to dream.

He dreamt he was swimming with Redcarp in a big lake, playing games and having fun.

Frog quickly woke up. When he thought about dreaming he was very happy.

天黑了。他想：我没有买到梦，今天晚上肯定也不会做梦的。

夜里真静，小青蛙轻轻呼吸着，一下睡着了。

小青蛙开始做梦了。

他做了一个大湖的梦。在梦里，他和红鲤鱼一起在湖中游来游去，一起做游戏。

他很快醒来，想着做的梦，心里甜蜜蜜的。

He was soon back asleep and he had a flying dream. In the dream Swan carried him on her back and they flew up in the blue sky, over the lake, over the mountains, to somewhere very very far away.

他又睡着了，又做了一个飞翔的梦。在梦里，白天鹅背着他，在蓝天上飞，越过湖水，越过高山，飞到了很远很远的地方。

And then, he had a swinging dream. He and Little White Bunny were on a swing, swinging, swinging. They swang so high that they could almost touch the clouds.

As the sky became light, Frog blinked and thought about his dreams and felt very happy. "It turns out I can dream wonderful things, too."

Still, there was one thing that he didn't understand: "I used not to be able to dream. Why can I dream now?"

他还做了一个秋千的梦。在梦里,他和小白兔在秋千上,荡呀,荡呀,荡到云朵里去了……

天亮时,他眨着眼睛,想着自己做过的梦。

"原来,我会做这么多好玩的梦呀!"小青蛙高兴极了。

可是,他还有点儿不明白:以前我不会做梦,为什么现在会做梦了呢?